GO AWAY

Written by Aisha Rodriguez
Illustrated by MadiLyn Sperry

Dedicated to KC Deane, who taught me more
about myself then I ever thought I needed to know.

I wake up early, very early! So early that the sun isn't even out yet.

But the birds
are chirping.

It doesn't matter what time it is; I just open my eyes, and I'm ready. Ready to sing, ready to dance.

Ready to play!

I run down the hall. I'm happy. I'm excited to start my day.

But the look on
Mommy's face says...

I go back to my room and try to be patient, but it's no fun.

I want to eat breakfast.

I want to watch TV.

I want to run. I WANT to go play outside!

I wait and wait, and finally...

If the sun is out and the birds are chirping, it must be okay.
I quickly run down the hall.

I'm so happy. I'm so excited to start my day!

But the look on
Mommy's face says...

I go back to my room. I make my bed. I tidy up, do a puzzle, and wait. I am patient, but it's no fun.

It feels so late.

Mommy comes into my room.
She's happy, she's excited.

"Honey, it's time to start your day!"

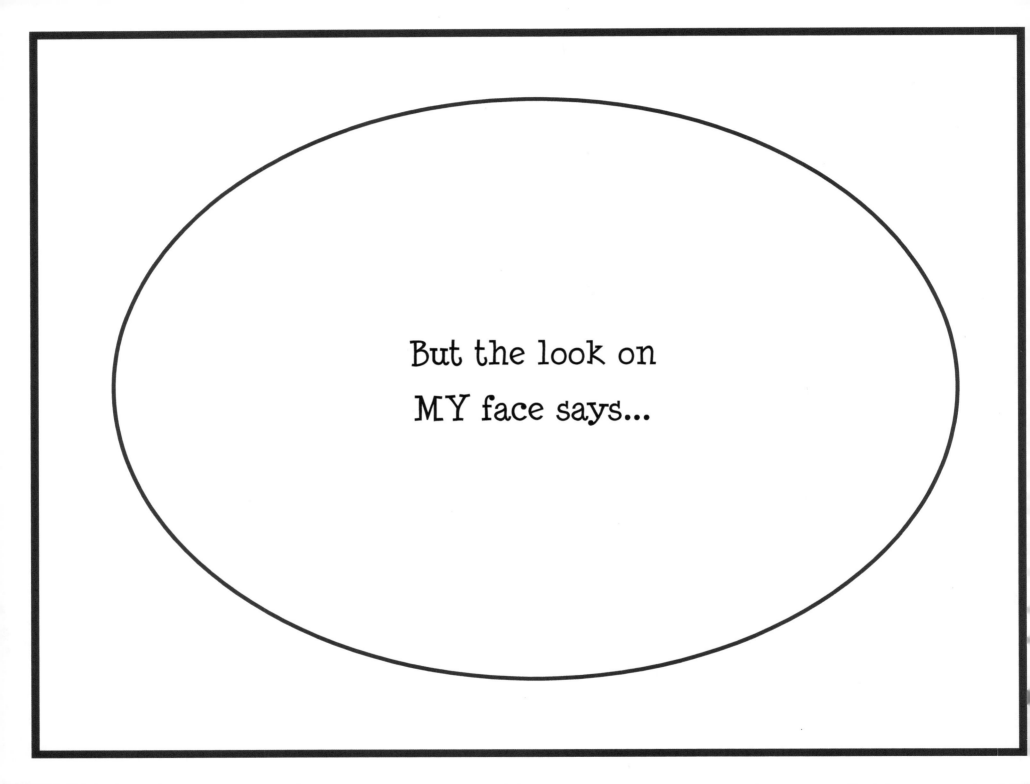

But the look on
MY face says...

Original pictures were sketched in graphite and traced in black ink pen. Once an outline was created, watercolor paint was applied from lightest color to darkest. Pen touch ups and small details were added once paint was dried.

A special thanks to family and friends who have loved, supported, and encouraged me throughout this process.

About the Author

Aisha Rodriguez was born in New York City, but now resides in Virginia with her family. Having been proudly raised in a military family, home is more a feeling than a place. Her most significant memories are with friends in Belgium and summers spent on Staten Island in Spanish Camp, a property formerly owned by the Spanish Naturopath Society. As a creative being, natural caregiver, teacher, and friend; Aisha has made a difference in the lives of many, but especially with the children and families she has worked with. Her stories are a way for her to celebrate joyous moments, embrace challenges, and take pride in some of her weakest moments. She hopes they will promote literacy and encourage quality time between children and their cherished adult/s.

About the Illustrator

MadiLyn Sperry is an artist living at the foot of the beautiful Utah Mountains in a small home with her daughter. She grew up on country land next to the ocean and has always had a love for beauty in life. Regardless of her surroundings, she has sand and salt in her heart. After graduating high school, she studied Fine Arts at Old Dominion University in Norfolk, VA where she cultivated many ways to express her love for life through art. Over the past few years, MadiLyn has been able to experience the world as a new and magical place through the eyes of her young daughter. This perspective has shaped much of her artistic views and passions.

CPSIA information can be obtained at www.ICGtesting.com
Printed in the USA
BVIW121816050720
583021BV00013B/161